Copyright © 2016 Concordia Publishing House
3558 S. Jefferson Avenue, St. Louis, MO 63118-3968
1-800-325-3040 • www.cph.org

Scripture quotation marked NKJV is taken from the New King James
Version®. Copyright © 1982 by Thomas Nelson, Inc. Used by permission.
All rights reserved.

Manufactured in USA   022100/300503

1 2 3 4 5 6 7 8 9 10   25 24 23 22 21 20 19 18 17 16

KATIE LUTHER

THE GRAPHIC NOVEL

Susan K. Leigh

Illustrated by Dave Hill

Mother of the Reformation

CONCORDIA PUBLISHING HOUSE · SAINT LOUIS

Zuhlsdorf

Black Cloister
Wittenberg

Brehna
Convent

Torgau

Erfurt

Nimbschen
Convent

This is the story of Katie Luther.

Born into a destitute family of noble lineage, Katharina von Bora grew up in a convent and was relegated to live as a nun in pre-Reformation Germany. She settled into a life of study and service at a nunnery near Nimbschen. Then, when Dr. Martin Luther's writings were spread throughout the land, some found their way into the hands of Katie and some other nuns at the nunnery. Those writings were the impetus for change. As much as Luther helped to reform the Church and spark sweeping change in Germany, he helped to transform a humble nun into a strong, intelligent, and inspiring leader in her own right.

“ My Katie is in all things so obliging and pleasing to me that I would not exchange my poverty for the riches of Croesus. ”

— Martin Luther

❖ Katie's Early Years

On January 29, 1499, in the old family manor near Lippendorf, a daughter—Katie—is born to Katharina Haubitz von Bora and Hans von Bora.

Katie had three brothers and one sister.

Death is a frequent visitor, and it casts a long shadow over the von Bora home.

In 1504, when Katie is only five years old, her mother dies.

Later that year, her father, Hans, remarries.

This is Margarethe von Bora, your stepmother.

The only real options for young ladies in medieval times are marriage, staying home to help take care of other family members, or going to a convent to become a nun. About a year after her mother died and around the time Katie turns six, it would have been time for her to start school. There probably was no school for girls in her village, so she is sent to a convent school in Brehna, about 30 miles from home.

Katie never lives with her siblings or parents again. Instead, she learns the routine and rigors of convent life.

Hard work, Katharina, is necessary to build character.

After three years in Brehna, nine-year-old Katie moves to Nimbschen to join the convent there. The abbess is Margaret Haubitz, a relative on her mother's side. Katie's aunt on her father's side, Magdalena von Bora, is a nun there too.

Welcome to our nunnery, Katie. I'm your Aunt Margaret.

Sister Katharina, do you vow to forsake the ways of the world?

In 1515, at the age of 16, Katie takes her vows to be a nun.

After that, Sister Katharina continues her studies, intending to one day become a teacher.

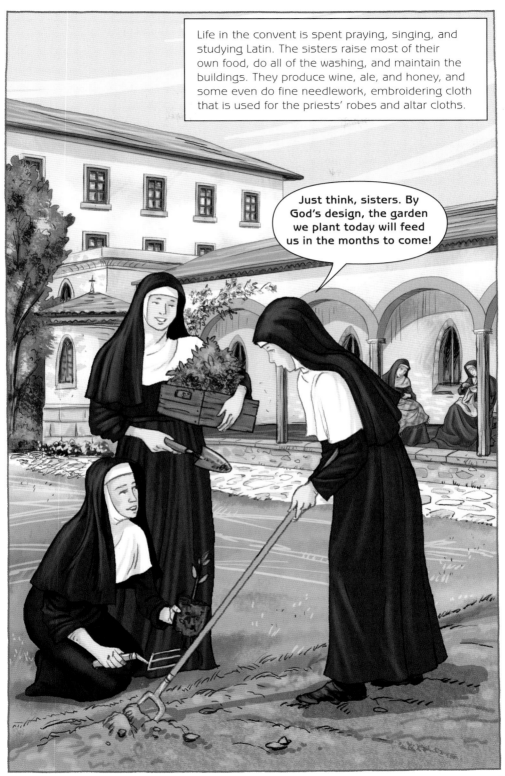

Life in the convent is spent praying, singing, and studying Latin. The sisters raise most of their own food, do all of the washing, and maintain the buildings. They produce wine, ale, and honey, and some even do fine needlework, embroidering cloth that is used for the priests' robes and altar cloths.

Just think, sisters. By God's design, the garden we plant today will feed us in the months to come!

The convent is situated amid a large estate where dozens of people live. The people work together, raising their own food and selling goods that provide income for the estate. The work Katie does at the convent helps prepare her for her future.

The Abbess

Women in the Middle Ages had little opportunity to have careers. A woman who came from a royal family or who married into a royal family would have wealth and status. But otherwise, the only way a woman could hold a position of power was to rise through the ranks in the convent. The position of abbess was an elected position. Other nuns in the convent would vote to choose who among them would have that opportunity of leadership and management.

17

By the time Katharina von Bora has taken her vows to be a nun, Dr. Martin Luther has spent years teaching, preaching, and writing at the university in Wittenberg. His Ninety-Five Theses, which he had posted on the doors of the Castle Church on October 31, 1517, had shaken Germany and the church in Rome to their cores. And the mighty Reformation Movement had begun.

Where is Martin?

Although Dr. Luther has powerful supporters in Germany, the church leaders oppose his writings. In 1520, he goes before the pope's representatives to state his case. He loses the case, and is charged with heresy, which means speaking out against the teachings of the church. Luther is excommunicated from the Roman Catholic Church. To some, he is the enemy. But to many thousands, Luther is the one who will lead them from oppression to religious and political freedom.

Every Christian who truly repents and confesses his sins to God is forgiven!

Of all of his accomplishments, one of Luther's greatest is his translation of the Bible into German, the language of the people. For the first time, anyone who can read has access to the Word of God.

Driven by his love for the Scriptures and his commitment to change, Martin Luther continues to publish essays about the Bible and its teachings and about the life that Christ would have believers live.

Somehow, Katie and the other nuns at the nunnery in Nimbschen obtain some of Luther's writings.

I agree with what Dr. Luther says here.

Because the pope declared Luther an enemy of the church, having any of his books is risky. It is especially dangerous for those who serve in church work—such as priests and nuns—to read his books or to attend his church services.

Despite the dangers, Katie and several of the other nuns in her convent decide to leave the order. They write to their family members asking for assistance.

Katie writes to her brother Hans, but he declines her request. She realizes she is on her own.

Dear Katie, I am sorry, but I simply cannot help you.

dangerous endeavor

Leaving a monastery or convent was a serious offense. Punishment was harsh and might even include execution!

Somehow, the plot by Katie and her sister nuns to escape is discovered—either someone turned them in or their letters were intercepted. They are severely punished for their betrayal. But their spirits are not broken.

Katie waits and hopes and prays for her release from the convent. Martin Luther's writings and preaching have begun a movement that cannot be suppressed.

Eventually, Aunt Magdalena relents and writes to Dr. Luther herself, asking him to help the nuns leave the order.

It is my Christian obligation to help these women.

Over the course of several weeks, after writing several letters back and forth, Luther and Magdalena devise a plan to help Katie and eleven other nuns escape from the convent.

I will send a man named Leonard.

Under cover of darkness on April 4, 1523, the night before Easter, Katie and the other nuns sneak out of their rooms and make their way to a door in the wall.

Outside the wall, Leonard Koppe, a merchant from Torgau, brings his wagon around, and ...

At a secret signal, the girls leave the convent, climb into the back of the wagon, cover themselves, and snuggle around the empty barrels. They had no belongings, no change of clothes, and no money.

Protected by the dark of night, Koppe, his nephew, and a third man lead the fugitives away from the convent and on toward Torgau and freedom. The journey was difficult because the roads were rough and the night was cold, but ...

they were free.

∾

The next morning, the freed nuns attend Easter mass at St. Mary's and hear Father Zwillig preach a sermon on Jesus' glorious resurrection.

Aided by sympathizers and generous townspeople, the nuns are given changes of clothing and food.

We don't know what will become of us, sisters, but at least we are free!

Two days after Easter, on Tuesday, the nuns are back on the road. This time to Wittenberg, where Dr. Luther has agreed to oversee their next move.

Some of the nuns return home to their families.

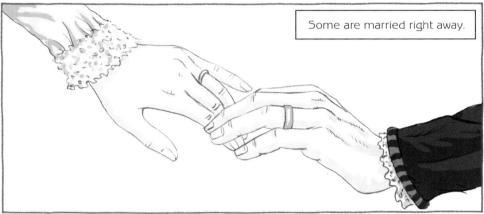

Some are married right away.

Some, like Katie, are employed by friends of Luther and others who support the Reformation. The former nuns help with housework and children.

As she settles into life in Wittenberg, Katie moves in with the Philipp Reichenbach family. Master Reichenbach is a lawyer and a university professor who goes on to become the mayor of Wittenberg in 1530. When Katie becomes a member of his household, beginning in the spring of 1523, she helps Mrs. Reichenbach run the house and care for the Reichenbach's young child. While living there, she meets Jerome Baumgartner, a wealthy young man from Nuremberg. Jerome and Katie soon begin a courtship, fall in love, and plan to marry.

Jerome returns home to tell his family about their plans, but they are not willing to let their son risk the family's reputation by his marrying a former nun. Jerome does not return to Wittenberg for Katie. A year later, he marries another woman.

Never! I will never marry!

Katie is heartbroken. And although she has several other suitors, including some who were selected just for her by Dr. Luther, she declines all offers of marriage.

Soon, Katie becomes a member of the Lucas Cranach household. There, she assists Barbara Cranach in the management of the busy estate and the care of the Cranach children. Katie becomes a beloved family friend and is treated like a daughter.

Lucas Cranach is a successful, talented businessman. The court painter, he is known for his portraits. He also owns a printing business and is Martin Luther's publisher.

The Cranach home is the largest house in Wittenberg, and it is to Katie's great advantage that she lives there. The Cranachs host many gatherings that are attended by important people who do business with Lucas or who are his friends. For instance, a certain Dr. Luther frequently visits the Cranach home.

The Rise of the Reformation

Although there had been attempts to reform the church for nearly a century, efforts in the early 1500s take firm hold. Theologians like Martin Luther (Germany), Erasmus (the Netherlands), Thomas More (England), and John Calvin (Switzerland) draw attention to corruption in the church in Rome. These learned men protest against church teachings and practices, such as that people can buy indulgences to earn forgiveness, that rich and powerful men can buy their way into leadership positions in the church, and that the church service is in Latin, which most people can't understand.

Vast changes are taking place throughout Europe in politics and industry. What makes the Reformation successful at this time is that improvements in printing technology have made all printed materials easier to produce and distribute. This means that Luther's writings become widely available throughout Europe. More and more people learn to read, and they are reading Luther's books. The public begins to question the church and side with the reformers.

▪ The Great Peasants' War

Most German people in the 1500s were peasants. With no education and no real opportunity to change that, they worked and worked, paid more and more taxes, and never, ever got ahead.

Peasant groups had tried uprisings in the past, hoping to improve their condition, but they were not successful. Then, when Luther was effective in challenging the church, they were inspired to revolt again— misunderstanding that the change Luther called for was for man's spiritual welfare, not his economic warfare.

There were hundreds of territories in Germany and Austria, and the peasant revolt during the mid-1520s was loosely organized. However, some groups did come together to write a list of requests called the Twelve Articles.

Luther approved of some of the articles, but not all of them. He encouraged both the peasants and the German princes to compromise. But compromise was difficult. There was too much emotion and too much history between them, and, in 1525, an all-out war ensued. The war was brutal. Luther tried to bring about peace, but he failed. Angry and frustrated, he wrote to the German princes, urging them to use force against the peasant uprising. The princes took his advice and sent their armies to kill the peasants.

The war was a disaster: an estimated 100,000 peasants and soldiers died, hundreds of homes and other buildings were destroyed, and Luther lost the support of a great number of his countrymen.

Martin does not plan to marry anyone. He is committed to the old church practice of priests and nuns not marrying, but his beliefs change.

As Luther studies the Bible, he comes to understand that there is no law against pastors marrying. So much do his thoughts about marriage change, that he writes about the blessings and benefits of pastors marrying, and he urges his friends to get married. The only thing left for him to do is to follow his own advice.

a surprising development

By now, Katie and Martin have known each other for more than two years. Luther was responsible for helping Katie and the eleven other nuns escape the convent, and he had also interceded for her with Jerome Baumgartner, though his attempt to arrange their marriage failed. He also tried to arrange her marriage to Dr. Caspar Glatz, but that was unsuccessful too.

Martin Luther feels compassion toward Katie, and he respects her intelligence and wisdom. They do not marry for love, but in time, they grow to love each other deeply.

The bride and groom celebrate their marriage at a formal dinner on June 27, 1525. The feast includes many of their friends and even Martin's parents, who are thrilled to attend.

Many offer their congratulations and send gifts and money to help the couple begin their life together.

But not all of Europe is pleased. Some of Luther's followers and even some of his friends are critical of the marriage. King Henry VIII of England is quite outspoken against the marriage, and he writes a disparaging letter to Luther telling him so.

" What you do in your house is worth as much as if you did it up in heaven for our Lord God. "   — Martin Luther

❖ Katie's Family Years

In time, the couple settles into a regular routine. Martin continues to lecture at the university, preach from the pulpit, write prolifically, and translate the Old Testament. He has no regular income, though. Martin relies on gifts of money and an allowance from Elector Frederick the Wise.

For years, Martin has lived in the Black Cloister, which belongs to Frederick. It becomes Katie's home now as well, and she takes over the management of the household.

The large building and grounds are in great need of attention. She makes it her first priority to make the house presentable for the many important visitors who come to see her husband.

Called "the Black Cloister" because of the color of the monk's clothes who live there, the large building is used by the university as a dormitory for up to forty students. It also includes lecture halls and living space. Construction on a chapel was begun but never finished.

Aunt Lena! We are so happy that you've come to live with us.

Katie's Aunt Magdalena von Bora, the former nun who was also part of the nunnery at Nimbschen, joins the household.

Thanks be to God, for He has given us a son. Dearest wife, I am a fortunate husband.

On June 7, 1526, baby Hans was born and, according to tradition, was baptized the same day.

Katie's tireless efforts at running the large estate require her to work very long hours. She often rises at four in the morning and works until well after sundown, which earns her the nickname "Morning Star" from her husband. Martin's loyal manservant, Wolf Sieberger, works with her.

Why, Katie? Why are you wearing mourning clothes? Has someone died?

With Katie running the household, Martin dedicates his time to writing and translating the Bible into the language of the people. He sometimes is so wrapped up in his work that he becomes worn down by physical ailment and slips into a depression. Katie tries to tease him out of his funk by putting on mourning clothes and moping around the house.

▪ The Plague

Europe is haunted by the plague, a gruesome disease that kills millions. As many as half of the people who contract the Black Death, as it is sometimes called, die within days of getting it. Outbreaks occur every few years from the 1340s to the mid-1660s. (Today, we know that the disease is carried by fleas, so we know how to prevent it. But in Katie Luther's day, the only way to fight it was by running away.)

When the plague comes to Wittenberg in the summer of 1527, many people leave town. The Luthers stay home, however, and open their house to their family and friends. Several of their guests are afflicted, and Katie and Aunt Lena help nurse them. Even baby Hans gets sick. The epidemic ends in the fall of that year. Wittenberg's residents return home and life returns to normal.

Our Lord has blessed us with a baby girl. Hans is here to meet his sister.

Elizabeth is born on December 10, 1527, and Martin and Katie are filled with joy.

Routine life in the Luther house includes frequent lectures and casual conversations. Students from the university gather around the family's dining table to discuss theology. These talks become a famous publication called Table Talks.

I do not know where God leads me, but I know that He is my guide.

After a short illness, perhaps related to the plague, baby Elizabeth dies in August of 1528.

In these times, when there are no antibiotics or other medical treatments, every illness is serious. Children often die at a very young age. The Luther family mourns Elizabeth's death. Yet they are confident that their beloved girl is forgiven of her sins and lives with Jesus in heaven.

The Black Cloister quickly becomes the gathering place for scholars and theologians. It is home to as many as thirty university students, as well as several servants, extended family members, and visitors. The Luther house is more like a hotel!

As the lady of the house, Katie is the manager, gardener, farmer, cook, nurse, cheese maker, beer brewer—and hostess!

In medieval times, children who need a home are taken in by relatives or are made to be servants. Some children are even abandoned in the streets.

Martin and Katie have a big house and even bigger hearts. They provide a home, care, and education to as many as eleven of their nieces and nephews.

Their own family grew as well. On May 4, 1529, Katie and Martin welcome baby Magdalena (Lena) into their family.

Martin continues his work as a writer and professor at the university in Wittenberg.

He also preaches regularly in the churches in and around Wittenberg.

Dr. Luther's work often takes him away from home. In 1530, he travels to Coburg and stays there the entire summer while the leaders of the new Lutheran Church meet with the leaders of the Roman Catholic Church in nearby Augsburg. Martin writes to Katie and their children regularly while he is away.

As the firstborn, Hans is allowed to spend a lot of time with his father. He plays quietly while his father works, but Herr Luther always has time to listen when his children have questions or are reciting their lessons.

Legend has it that Martin Luther introduced the tradition of the Christmas tree. This may or may not be so, but the Luthers love St. Nicholas Day, Christmas Eve, and Christmas Day, and take the opportunity to give praise to the Christ Child.

Martin learns from letters the sad news about his father's death on May 29, 1529, and about his mother's death on June 30, 1530.

But even as one life ends, another begins. On November 9, 1531, the Luther family's second son, Martin, is born.

The Luther family loves to entertain, and one of the things they love to do the most is celebrate happy occasions.

When Martin turns one, they celebrate with a gathering of family and friends. And when Hans turns six, they feast on cake, enjoy music, play games, and make the day one to remember!

The Black Cloister

On February 4, 1532, Elector John the
Steadfast formally gives the Black Cloister
and its grounds to Martin and Katie. Now
that they own the home, they can do more
than just make repairs to the rundown
property. Martin and Katie begin making major
improvements, including building a brewhouse
and a guesthouse, greatly expanding the
gardens, and renovating the house itself.
These renovations include building a new entry
to the house (the well-known Luther Portal),
rebuilding public rooms, adding bedrooms for
the children and Aunt Lena, repairing the roof,
and adding windows and a basement.

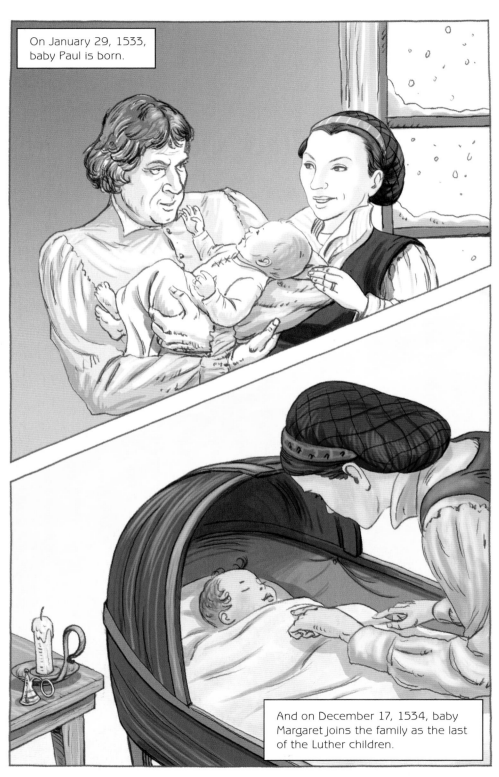

On January 29, 1533, baby Paul is born.

And on December 17, 1534, baby Margaret joins the family as the last of the Luther children.

Life in the convent had been good training for life in the Black Cloister. When Katie became a wife and mother and manager of a large household, she already knew how to run a large estate.

Her friends know her for her hospitality and her generous and warm welcome to visitors. At various times, especially when Martin and his fellow reformers were traveling around Germany, Katie opens her home to the wives and children of the reformers. Some stay for months on end. At other times, like when the plague ravages Wittenberg, Katie and Martin turn the Black Cloister into a hospital with Katie, Aunt Lena, and the servants offering medical care.

Besides providing a place to stay, Katie constantly works to prepare meals for their guests. She makes good use of the land around the home by planting kitchen gardens and raising goats. She also acquires farms outside of the city where more food is grown and dairy cows are kept. In addition to providing food for the forty or more people who might be living at the Black Cloister at any one time, the farms are investment property that provided an income for the Luther family. Should Katie outlive her husband, she would need a way to support herself and her children.

Martin is called away from home again and again to deal with church business.

In February 1537, he travels to Smalcald where he and others plan to discuss the official statements of belief the new church body plans to adopt.

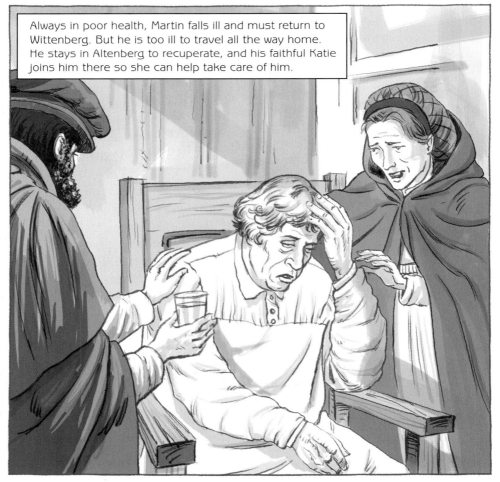

Always in poor health, Martin falls ill and must return to Wittenberg. But he is too ill to travel all the way home. He stays in Altenberg to recuperate, and his faithful Katie joins him there so she can help take care of him.

After years of hard work, Katie and Martin plan to slow down. They visit their beautiful home at Zuhlsdorf on the Elbe River, away from the hustle and bustle of Wittenberg. But they do not move from the Black Cloister.

My heart has grown so cold about the changes in Wittenberg that I would rather stay here at Zuhlsdorf.

That same year, 1537, Katie's beloved Aunt Lena falls ill. And after a lifetime of serving God and her family, Magdalena von Bora passes away.

Meanwhile, Hans, the oldest of the Luther children, continues to advance in his schooling. He leaves home to attend a prestigious school in Torgau.

On November 1, 1539, Katie suffers the grief of a miscarriage. Within weeks, she becomes quite ill, and by the end of January 1540, Katie is near death.

Her husband and friends pray for her and nurse her as best they can with the common medicines of the day. She gradually improves, but her recovery takes weeks.

Martin Luther has seen much and worked hard throughout his life. As he grows older, he has less patience for the problems in Germany and in the church. He becomes irritated and bitter about the way people lead their lives and about disagreements in the church.

To make matters worse, their thirteen-year-old daughter, Magdalena, falls ill. On September 20, 1542, she dies in her father's arms. The family is deeply grieved, and Martin's health continues to deteriorate. For years, he has been troubled by stomach problems, headaches, and a bad leg. Grief is surely a factor in his decline.

Despite these things, Dr. Luther continues to work and to serve the church. In January 1546, he travels to Eisleben—his birthplace—to help settle a dispute between two property owners. His three sons take the trip with him.

the end comes

On February 17, Luther falls ill with chest pains. The doctors use all of their skill to treat him, but they are not successful.

Dr. Martin Luther dies in the early morning of February 18, 1546. His last words are, "Father, into Your hands I commend my spirit. You have redeemed me, faithful God."

"I have commended you to God and to my most gracious Lord, along with the little children." — Martin Luther

❖ Katie's Later Years

How much sadness can Katie endure?

She lost her mother when she was just five. She buried two of her dear little girls. She lost her dear Aunt Lena, who was her friend and substitute mother. And now … Katharina von Bora Luther says farewell to her beloved husband.

"He gave so much of himself in service not only to one town or to one country, but to the whole world. Yes, my sorrow is so deep that no words can express my heartbreak, and it is humanly impossible to understand what state of mind and spirit I am in. … I can neither eat nor drink, not even sleep. … God knows that when I think of having lost him, I can neither talk nor write in all my suffering."

After Martin's death, Katie and her children try to resume normal life. But how can things ever be the same? Katie's dear husband is gone, and her children have no father.

Nevertheless, meals must be prepared and the people living in their home must be cared for.

In his will, Martin provides for Katie and their children, but his will does not allow for them to stay at the Black Cloister.

Instead, she is to inherit their other property, as well as all of the debt.

Martin never made much money; instead, he relied on help from the elector and his friends.

Katie begs Martin's friends to help her keep her home, but many of them ignore her requests.

Eventually, Katie's brother Hans von Bora is appointed as her guardian.

His assistance means Katie and her children can stay at the Black Cloister for the time being.

Europe is constantly at war because the princes and governments battle for power and property. In the summer of 1546, the war between the Protestant princes and the Catholic emperor reaches Wittenberg. Katie and her children join the throngs of people who flee for their own safety. The Luther family's faithful servant, Wolf, stays behind as the family seeks shelter in Magdeburg, about 47 miles away.

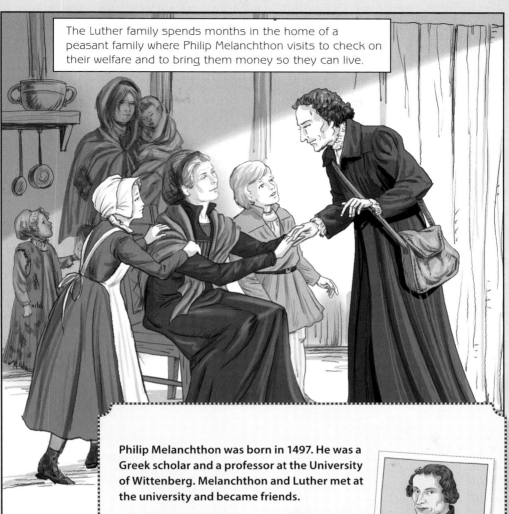

The Luther family spends months in the home of a peasant family where Philip Melanchthon visits to check on their welfare and to bring them money so they can live.

Philip Melanchthon was born in 1497. He was a Greek scholar and a professor at the University of Wittenberg. Melanchthon and Luther met at the university and became friends.

Melanchthon is considered a great reformer, second only to Martin Luther. He made many important contributions to the church, including the Augsburg Confession and the organization and explanation of Reformation beliefs. And he represented Luther at important meetings such as the Diet of Augsburg. In addition to his work in the church, he reformed the entire education system in Germany, which became the standard for schools throughout all of Europe.

After Luther died, Melanchthon became a key leader of the Lutheran Church until his own death in 1560.

devastated by war

Katie and her children return to Wittenberg in the spring of 1547, only to leave again a month later when war rages once more. This time, they decide to go to Denmark, where the king is a good friend to Katie, but the roads are not safe enough for the journey. The Luthers find a temporary home in Braunschweig.

During the few weeks that Katie is away from home, she receives several letters with news about Wittenberg. The city was devastated by the war. Although the city walls protected the Black Cloister, the university, and other buildings, all of the buildings and property outside the wall were destroyed, including Katie's farm, livestock, and gardens. Many of Katie's friends are imprisoned, including Elector John Frederick and Lucas Cranach. And the saddest news is that Martin's faithful, beloved servant Wolf Sieberger has died.

Exhausted and penniless, Katie and her children return home to the Black Cloister instead of continuing their journey to Denmark.

Over time, the gardens are replanted. Katie takes in boarders as a source of income she desperately needs to keep the estate running. University students live there and professors use some of the rooms as lecture halls.

Katie remains the Morning Star, and her sons Martin and Paul and her daughter Margaret remain at home where they care for their mother and for one another.

With support of Duke Albrecht of Prussia, her son Hans goes to Konigsberg in East Prussia to study law.

Although she is successful in keeping boarders at the Black Cloister, the economics of running a large estate and caring for her family become burdensome.

I must have a very good price for this goblet. It is of great value.

Because there is very little income, the Luther household must find money somewhere so Hans can stay in college. Katie finally decides to sell a treasured gold goblet that she and Martin had received as a wedding gift.

She continues to beg Luther's friends to honor his memory by helping her. Only a few actually do. Some continue to ignore her.

Others are just as affected by the wars and plagues as Katie and her family.

The years of hard work begin to wear on her.

Her family insists that she hire more help, but when Katie discovers that a maid is stealing from the family, she refuses to hire more help.

The Plague returns

In the summer of 1552, the plague again ravages Wittenberg and some of the Black Cloister's residents are afflicted. Katie nurses her boarders as best as she can, but the years of toil and her age mean that she can't keep up with the work.

Katie, her sons, and daughter Margaret decide to leave Wittenberg and flee to Torgau, leaving the threat of illness and death behind.

Throughout the years since her husband's death, Katie's primary concern was the well-being of her family. Despite legal hurdles, she fought tirelessly—and successfully—for the right to stay in the Black Cloister. Some of Wittenberg's leaders wanted to split up the children, to send them to other people who would support them. Katie won that dispute as well.

When wars and plagues came to Wittenberg, Katie's first thought was to protect her children from danger. She did that by taking them to a safer location.

The road to Torgau is rain-soaked and dangerous. Katie holds the reins tight, but when the horse is spooked, she loses control and the wagon crashes.

She falls hard, landing in a ditch, and is knocked unconscious.

Katie's injuries brought on paralysis and fever. She lingered for three months, praying constantly. Her daughter, eighteen-year-old Margaret, and her landlady attend to her as best as they can.

a life of godliness

Katharina Luther dies on December 20, 1552. She is buried the next day in St. Mary's Church in Torgau.

Her funeral is attended by many displaced students and professors, who have also fled to Torgau to escape the plague in Wittenberg. Also present are her three sons, Hans, Martin, and Paul (and his fiancée, Anna), and her daughter Margaret.

Philip Melanchthon, her husband's good friend and the leader of the Lutheran Church in Germany, writes her obituary, asking that she be honored for her godliness.

Katharina
von Bora
1499 - 1552

The Legacy of Katie Luther

Intelligent, brave, and tireless in her work, Katie loved her family and had a deep, unshakable faith in the Lord God.

Katie Luther's lasting legacy may well be her role as a woman. Along with her husband, she helped to form the modern view of the wife's role in marriage and home.

What became of Katie and Martin's children?

Hans went on to practice law. He married Elisabeth Cruciger and they had one daughter. Hans died in 1575 at the age of 49.

Martin studied theology, although he did not enter into the ministry. He married Anna Heilinger. Martin died in 1565 at the age of 34.

Paul became a university professor and physician. He was a sought-after doctor. Paul married Anna von Warbeck just a few weeks after Katie died. They had six children. He died in 1593 at the age of 60.

Margaret married nobleman George von Kunheim. Margaret had nine children, but only three outlived her. She died in 1570 at the age of 36.

If you would like to learn more about Katie Luther:

Katharina von Bora: A Reformation Life, Rudolf K. Markwald, Marilynn Morris Markwald (Concordia Publishing House, 2002)

The Mother of the Reformation: The Amazing Life and Story of Katharine Luther, Ernst Kroker, transl. Mark E. DeGarmeaux (Concordia Publishing House, 2013)

Luther: Echoes of the Hammer, Susan K. Leigh (Concordia Publishing House, 2011)

Martin Luther wrote *Luther's Small Catechism with Explanation* (Concordia Publishing House, 2005) in order to teach the basics of the Christian faith.

These books explain what Lutherans believe:

Lutheranism 101 (Concordia Publishing House, 2015)

The Lutheran Study Bible (Concordia Publishing House, 2009)

Concordia: The Lutheran Confessions (Concordia Publishing House, 2009)

"For with the heart
one believes unto
righteousness."
Romans 10:10 NKJV

SUSAN K. LEIGH is an editor and author who lives in a small town in Illinois. She began her career in publishing as a contributing writer for her high school yearbook, worked as a newspaper reporter during college, and then as a magazine editor for a dozen years. After a three-year stint as an advertising copywriter, she began a day job as a book editor and has stayed put.

Susan is the author of several children's picture books, including twelve titles in the best-selling God, I Need to Talk to You series and *Luther: Echoes of the Hammer*.

When she isn't writing, Susan is knitting, gardening, or playing with her grandkids.

DAVE HILL graduated from Glasgow School of Art in 1983 and began his career as a painter with exhibitions in Glasgow, Edinburgh, Liverpool, and London.

He then worked in the video game industry for ten years as a concept artist producing character and environment designs in both 2D and 3D.

As a freelance illustrator, Dave's passion is children's books, although he has also illustrated comic books, storyboards, greeting cards, and product packaging.

Dave produces most of his work digitally, although he still dabbles in traditional media, painting in oils and watercolor.

He lives in Scotland with his wife, Anne, and their two children, David and Amy.

www.davehillsart.co.uk